The Trouble with Gran

For Rosie, Jim and the boys
(who also come from a tropical planet!)

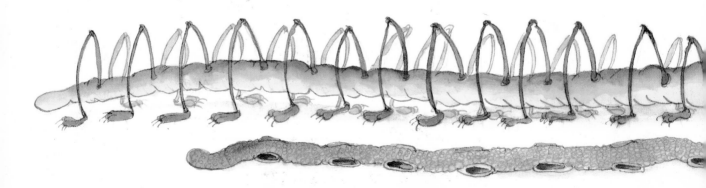

The Trouble with Gran

Babette Cole

G. P. Putnam's Sons   New York

COLE 1988

The trouble with Gran is . . .

None of the other senior citizens
suspected a thing . . .

until our teacher tried to organize
a trip to
Wettisburg
for them,
as our school
project!

"But we want to go somewhere hot and exciting!" said Gran.

"Sit down and be quiet," said Teacher.

Wettisburg in January was awful.

Gran started to act up!

At the pier there was an Old Time Music Hall . . .

Gran did not like the singing!

. . . and there was a Glamorous Grandma contest . . .

... Gran cheated of course!

She really livened up the fun fair!

We were asked to leave the amusement arcade!

On the Lunar Landscape Tour
Gran met some friends.

She took them out
for a snack!

So we missed the bus home.

Teacher blamed Gran!

"We've had enough of this!" said Gran.
"Fasten your seat belts!"

We zoomed toward Gran's planet! . . .

and landed just in time
for carnival!

Gran did the Limbo . . .

. . . and climbed a bloomernut tree.

No one wanted to leave
but Gran had to get home
to feed the cat.

We landed in the school playground with a bump!

Mom and Dad took Gran home. "You're too old for that sort of thing anymore," they said.

Gran didn't care!

And when she
got home
she opened
her own
travel
agency . . .

. . . in Dad's garage!

First published by William Heinemann Ltd
First impression
Printed in England

Library of Congress Cataloging-in-Publication Data
Cole, Babette.
    The trouble with Gran.
Summary: Gran, who is secretly an extraterrestrial
being, livens up a trip to the seaside taken by a
group of school children and senior citizens.
[1. Grandmothers—Fiction.   2. Extraterrestrial
beings—Fiction]   I. Title.
PZ7.C6734Tq 1987   [E]   86-25519
ISBN 0-399-21428-3